THE BOOK OF
MINI-SAGAS

THE BOOK OF MINI-SAGAS

from the

TELEGRAPH
SUNDAY MAGAZINE

competitions

With an introduction by
BRIAN ALDISS

ALAN SUTTON
1985

ALAN SUTTON PUBLISHING
BRUNSWICK ROAD · GLOUCESTER

First published 1985

British Library Cataloguing in Publication
Data

The Book of mini-sagas
I. Aldiss, Brian W.
823′.01′08[FS] PR6051.L3

ISBN 0-86299-269-9

Typesetting and origination by
Alan Sutton Publishing Limited
Photoset Garamond 12/12
Printed in Great Britain by
The Guernsey Press Company Limited
Guernsey, Channel Islands

CONTENTS

INTRODUCTION

Ours is a century which,
in trying to abolish art, spawns new
art forms — from clerihews to
computer games. Now here comes the
mini-saga! What are mini-sagas?
They are hot-rod versions of the
Odyssey; a cross between graffiti and
prose haiku; megalosaurus-sized
mouthfuls, designed to tease
reader and writer alike.

Regarding the form of the mini-saga, there are
three rules only. The story must be fifty
words long, neither more nor less (the above
paragraph consists of fifty words, just to give
you an idea); the title must be no more than
fifteen; and a story should be conveyed, not
simply a mood or anecdote.

The mini-sagas were launched as a
competition in 1982, in the *Telegraph
Sunday Magazine*, with great success. John
Anstey, the Magazine's editor, and I did not
expect so many people would wish to play;
but received over 32,000 entries. The
judges' lives were dislocated for weeks. In
1985, in collusion with the BBC Radio 4
'Today Programme', we ran our competition
again (with alluring prizes). This time, we
received nearly 50,000 entries — 48,435 to
be precise.

Among our judges have been Frank Muir,
Ian McEwan, Maggie Gee, and Brian Redhead,

Among our judges have been Frank Muir, Ian McEwan, Maggie Gee, and Brian Redhead, ably assisted by David Holloway, Literary Editor of the *Daily Telegraph*.

But to judge by the evidence, the lives of the competitors have been even more dislocated. They bombarded us with violence, death and nuclear holocausts by the minibucket-load; or with uplift . . . God intervened personally in domestic affairs hundreds and hundreds of times.

While testing out the idea of the mini-saga, I came to believe that it was at its most effective when it gave to a general truth a local habitation and a name:

HAPPINESS AND SUFFERING

The doors of the amber palace
closed behind the young king.
For 20 years he dallied with his
favourite courtesan. Outside, the
land fell into decay. Warlords
terrorised the population.
Famine and pestilence struck,
of which chronicles still tell.
The king emerged at last.
He had no history to relate.

The title seems rather too abstract; but when the story is read, the title is seen to illuminate the implied meanings in the text. Suggestions are better than bludgeons.

Not all of the contestants agreed with my approach. They used the mini-saga for fears and confessions. The results were highly entertaining and, in the mass, exhausting. The first competition's winner, however, *Paper Marriages* a beautiful story by Carol Burns, allowed both time and feeling into its narrow realm. R.S. Ferm's *Different Values*, winner of the second competition, contained a strong sense of the world's variety. From which it may be deduced that telling any story – not merely a mini-saga – entails something more than listing a series of violent and morose events.

National obsessions were revealed, from the dread of being run over by a double-decker bus to a love-hatred of cats. There were ten mentions of cats to every one of dogs. Man-eating budgerigars also featured. I listed the following popular themes, not in any order: death in the home; murder everywhere; nuclear war (often treated nostalgically, with an archetypal last sentence, 'And then silence reigned once more'); cats; adultery (so much more interesting than cats); doppelgangers; being born; The Wife; The Husband; ageing; and the difficulty of writing mini-sagas.

The very frequency of some themes rules them out. As any editor will tell you, the Adam and Eve story rewritten is one to avoid. However, this volume contains a variant, complete with perfect title, by Mrs M. Gillies Watson. It is very funny.

But funniness *per se* was not always a great success, though there were many good new jokes set down.

My least favourite ploy is bathos, the letdown. In fifty words one has no space for inflation, never mind deflation. Of all bathos, erotic bathos is the least satisfactory. For example:

DOMESTIC CATASTROPHE

He was aware of how closely
she watched him. Tonight was
something special. Suddenly, he
seized her in his arms and
began fondling her as he had
always wished. She purred
in response. He could tell she was
aroused. Then she scratched him.
He threw her down – nasty
family moggie.

Another popular let-down which wins my
wooden spoon is the story ending 'But it was all
a dream'. In those cases, reality is a waiting
waste-paper basket.

The list of favourite themes was much the
same for children as for adults, with The Father
and The Mother replacing The Wife and The
Husband. Niall Wyllie's jolly *I Think My Dad
must be Superman* is an exception to the rule that
fathers are despised; more typical is Kathryn
Wheeler's Dad in *The Last Time we had Peanut
Butter*.

Children did come up with one pervasive
theme: the video game. I lost count of the
number of wars which broke out in the first
sentence, but proved in the last to be contained
within a Space Invaders machine. Often the
teller was trapped inside the video game, like
the characters in the film *Tron*.

Children, more than adults, went for science-
fictional themes, but it is difficult to work up
atmosphere in fifty words. Another gambit

which failed was the shooting told by the chap who got killed.

Children venture into faction more often than adults. Faction is a blend of fiction and fact. Most successful were the story called *Toyah's Struggle* and the harrowing tale of Sarah Feltham's love for Adam Ant. Although they did not win prizes in the competition, I am glad to print them here.

Most surprising was the preoccupation with the supernatural. Astrology was not mentioned, but ghosts were. People came back from the dead. As firm a belief was shown in the after-life as in superstitious omens. Church-yards figured large. Britain is alive and well, and living in the eighteenth century.

There is no rule against rhyming, except the rule of nature, which says that verse is − for most people − more difficult than prose. One or two verses are included here, as well as a palindromic mini-saga, welcome for its originality.

Titles are an integral part of a mini-saga; the roof to the building. Many submitted titles hectored, and did not promise well, though they had a weird fascination in their own right: 'The Boy Bastard with Wild Hate Magic is Thwarted by the Mystery of Love'; 'The Hateful Impact of his own Carelessness upon an Unrepentant Sinner'; 'Behind Every Dead Man there is a Woman who Pushed him Too Far'. Whatever follows such pronouncements is almost bound to be an anti-climax.

Thanks must go to all who submitted entries, from Kensington Palace to Dartmoor and Broadmoor. Many schools submitted entries − Northumberland putting up a particularly heavy barrage. Many individuals

sent in multiple entries, often of high stand-
ard. There the laurels go to James Cawthorn,
the artist, and Susan Thorpe, as these pages
show.

Oxford   BRIAN ALDISS
August 1985

LOVED ONES

PAPER MARRIAGE: THE TALE OF TWO NOVELISTS

At their wedding, she
carried carnations.
They published novels.
At 23 she was unfaithful; at 26
he was unfaithful. They lived
in separate countries, met
in dreams and unwritten
novels as glass characters;
they carried babies,
alimony cheques, bloody
carnations. United in death,
they sit in print on
library shelves.

Carol Burns

LONDON W1

— *1982 1ST PRIZE – ADULT* —

TO BE CAREFUL,
TO BE CARING

When she walked, I watched.
When she talked, I listened.
Lighting her cigarettes
was an act of love. And a
betrayal, for they killed her.
I was careful, Jennie. You
were my only addiction. I was
afraid to ask you
to be careful, too.
Because I might have lost
you.

James Cawthorn

LONDON W10

JOHN AND MARY – OR LIFE, TRANSITORY AS SUMMER LIGHTNING IN A STORMY UNIVERSE

Pale blue sky, golden motes
through shiny new leaves,
When John met Mary

Sultry, ochre streaked sky,
dusty cobwebbed blackberries,
When John and Mary had Jane

Crystal air,
russet leaves crunching,
scarves flying,
When Jane left John and Mary

Bare boughs,
hard ploughed fields,
When John and Mary left Jane.

Pauline Amendt

COBHAM

CARE IN THE COMMUNITY OF MEN AND BIRDS

The boy was locked up for
screaming like a parrot.
At forty they released him.
'Go back to the community,
where you belong.'
He went home
hooting like an owl.
His mother cried:
'Go back to where you really
belong!' and turned to
kiss her parrot, which
talked like a man.

Maggie Gee

— *COMMISSIONED EXAMPLE* —

DEATHS
BY MISADVENTURE

He held the frayed kettle flex.
She was careless with
electricity, switching on with
wet hands. He dipped the
plug in water.
In town a car braked too late.
The doorbell rang.
'Make yourself some tea,' said
the police sympathetically.
With trembling, sweat-soaked
hands he plugged in and
switched on.

Pam Winterbottom

SUTTON COLDFIELD

DARK LOVE – A FAMILY SAGA OF MIXED EMOTIONS (WARNING: EXPLICIT EXCERPTS MAY AFFECT THE SQUEAMISH)

The post-copulative ecstasy, experienced by a very young Black Widow after devouring her first husband, dwindled somewhat as she knitted and spun in anticipation of a Happy Event. Eventually, fifty, adorable, little furry spiders appeared. 'Oh!' she gasped delightedly, 'You're just like your father!' and she ate them ALL up.

Melody Drake-Lee

ROSS-ON-WYE

— 1985 RUNNER UP – ADULT —

BLIND DATE, BLIND PANIC, BLIND . . .

Only one hour to go!
Neither by overloading
the mascara, nor with cheeks
hollowed, was she seductive
or svelte. She tossed aside
garments too tight, too
young and crammed on a wide
brimmed hat. Thank God for
flattering shadows!

* * *

He approached, red flower in
button hole, lightly tapping his
white stick.

Heather Deighton

LONDON NW1

WILL HE ESCAPE
TRUE LOVE?

She touched his knees, fiddled
his collar, stared into his
eyes, melting. Silent, he stared
elsewhere, jerked his head.
An old man puzzled over the
juke-box. The young man
leaped up, helped, chatted.
When the old man joined them
she stared at him instead, eyes
ice, mouth a thin line.

P. J. Kavanagh

SOME ARE BORN RESPECTABLE; SOME ACHIEVE RESPECTABILITY; OTHERS HAVE RESPECTABILITY THRUST UPON THEM

A lime-haired punk walked past
daily, to meet a puce-tipped,
raven-spiked punkette.
Always, they kissed. Smoked.
Slept. Together.
But then she rinsed out the dye.
Went to an office daily,
hospital nightly. Saved Money.
And even in labour,
losing the brat gradually, she
wanted to be Alone.

Sara Pennell

FERNDOWN

Age 15

22

SHOW-BIZ

'MY SONG GOES ROUND THE WORLD – TO RETURN LIKE A BOOMERANG'

She was the great pop singer of
1962. Everyone knew her
'In Cahoots with Joy'. Then
came the GROUPS . . .
For years she worked
the Outback and Blackpool on
drugs and sordid lovers.
Now – marriage, new records.
And a small son. Singing
her old song . . .
Again she was in cahoots
with joy.

Philip K. Dunn

BOMBAY

THERE COMES
A TIME WHEN
THE MUSICALS HAVE
TO STOP!

'Evita!'
'Hello, Dolly.'
'How's The Boy Friend? Gone
With The Wind?'
'Listen, My Fair Lady, he's in
the South Pacific with Pal
Joey in a Showboat.'
'Oh, there's The Sound of
Music. It's a Fiddler
On The Roof
with The Merry Widow.
They're Playing Our Song —
Wild, Wild Women!'
'Cats!'

Shiela Cave

LONDON SW1

X-CERTIFICATE

The lights dimmed.
The titles rolled.
She was beautiful. She wanted
him. He gripped her
stocking sheathed thighs,
sliding up her short black skirt.
Moaning ecstatically she
clawed her blouse, buttons
ricocheted from hot breasts.
A menacing voice hissed behind
their writhing bodies, 'Not 'ere
mate, watch the bloody film!'

S.D. Smart

EDINBURGH

THE
HISTORY OF
ROCK AND ROLL
CONSIDERED
AS A
STORM-TOSSED
SAILBOAT
RACE

The Fifties started well but got
stuck up a backwater.
Spirit of Hope, the sixties
boat, springs a leak and sinks;
the survivors man the
lifeboats.
The crew of the good ship
Punk mutiny.
That old tramp *Disco*'s slick
fouls the race.
Maybe it's time someone sent
up a flare?

Jeremy Hoyland

FRINTON-ON-SEA

STATESIDE: THE EPIC BESTSELLER WHICH SHOCKED AMERICA. NOW A MAJOR TELEVISION SERIES

Millionaire widower Buck,
father of psychotic Junior
and drug addict Diamond,
marries nymphomaniac
Opal, mistress of his illegitimate
son Dean, incestuously involved
with Diamond. Junior,
despising everybody except his
dead mother, murders Dean,
rapes Opal and is
certified insane. Diamond
overdoses. Opal becomes frigid.
Buck, realising life's futility,
shoots himself.

Tony Bromfield

BROCKENHURST

THE END OF
SOMEONE'S
TETHER

Harold Wall was taciturn.
He was not pleased when he
found himself clutching a
would-be suicide at the top of
Dead Man's Leap, while the
police shouted: 'Keep him
in conversation 'til we
get to you.' 'What's
your job?' tried Harold.
'I hosted a chat show on —'
Harold let go.

Frances Rhodes

HAMBLEDON

TOYAH'S STRUGGLE

Toyah's fame has come after
many years of struggling.
She became a drink addict and a
punk. Her school friend
thought she was mad. Specialist
treatment helped her lisp.
All the years of agony
have payed off for now she is a
brilliant singer and actress
and a cult hero.

Katy Leigh

Age 15

INSIDE INFORMATION: HOW TO MAKE A MILLION. LESSON 22

There was this pop star and he
hadn't been selling many
records recently and like he was
finished, you know. And he
died. Drugs an' that.
And naturally his records sold in
millions again. Actually,
between you and me, he'd had a
haircut and lived quietly
in Esher.

Stephen Lochey

ADAM ANT

Adam Ant nestled snugly into a
corner of my heart, especially
reserved for only him in
1981. Since then I've felt that
between myself and him, a
bond has sprung up, though its
probably very one-sided. Now
he's on the verge of
marriage and who cares
about life anyway.

ADAM ANT'S NEST

Once upon 1982 I was in love
with Adam Ant. He meant
everything to me, he was all
that mattered in life.
Then I read the 'Star' and
my dreams were shattered by
some girl so I attempted
suicide. Sadly I didn't succeed
in killing myself.
Tell him for me.

(The above story is totally true, *no lies, no
'additives', just the truth. I love Adam Ant
more than I've ever loved anyone in my life.)*

ADAM ANT RULES
OK?

Once upon an 'Abbey Hall' I
fell for a Sheaffer (not pen),
then this fickle 'knight' turned
up with a girl on his steed,
so I stampeded the city with
a band of yanks. But Adam,
my hero, remained faithful,
plastered over my walls,
surfacing victorious yet again.
(Three cheers!)

(with writing disguised)

Sarah Feltham

PLYMOUTH

Age 15

THE MAN WHO RULED THE WORLD FORGOT TO BRIEF HIS P.R. ASSISTANT

All men shook his hand.
Leo dazzled, smiled and
tipped a million pounds.
The sick touched him, hoping.
Leo took a trip into the
Amazon to find himself. His
throat was parched. He clutched
a sweaty million.
'Get me some water!'
The uncertain natives stared.
'I'm Leo!'
'Who?' they chorused.

Sarah Weatherall

BISHOPS WALTHAM

DOMESTIC

THE UNWANTED PRESENT

I don't know why, but in every
park there's always a single
small glove on the ground.
I wonder how many mothers of
young children have had to
throw away the other, and
how many children have
celebrated ridding themselves
of those awful looking gloves
made for them by aunts.

Alex Allinson

RICHMOND

Age 16

THE
DEATH TOUCH

When a daughter went
away to college, she reluctantly
left her plants and her
goldfish in her mother's care.
Once the daughter telephoned
and her mother confessed
that the plants and
the goldfish had died.
There was a prolonged silence.
Finally, in a small voice,
the daughter asked,
'How's Dad?'

Dawn Hunt

STAFFORD

— *1985 RUNNER UP – UNDER 18* —

LIFE
AND NUMBERS

Once upon a time
there was
just Me.
I soon realised there were
three of us, then gradually
four. At last there were just
the two of us. All at once four
of us. Suddenly just the two
of us again. Now there is
only Me
as in the beginning.

Frances Politzer

TRUMPINGTON

A
LASTING BOND

They had married in haste.
Now they were repenting at
leisure and action for divorce
had started. But today their
child was in hospital.
They stood by his bed as
he opened his eyes.
'Mummy, Daddy, don't leave
me,' he said.
'Of course we won't,' they
replied, and meant it.

Austin F. Janes

LEIGHTON BUZZARD

A CASE OF
WANTON
ATTENTION

It wasn't as if he'd
known her very long. A few
months at most.
Despite her continued cries and
sobs he persisted. Her
clothes lay scattered and
soiled. Her nudity exposed, his
pent up emotions now
overflowed. He was going to
have his way.
His daughter's nappy would
be changed!

Dr J. Macrae

WOKING

LIVING-IN

We moved house, met
the neighbours, eyed their
children. Commonplace people
leading commonplace lives.
'Come and see my train,'
said the child.
'And stamp collection.
And the rabbit up in my room.'
Then he whispered, in
exquisite intimacy: 'And my
grandpa's got two grandmas.
One lives in the attic.'

Caroline van Tienen

BURY ST EDMUNDS

A USELESS BUY

No fun sitting here at the
bottom of the pool writing
letters.
The paper is soggy, and the
envelopes keep getting
stuck.
And my rheumatism is worse.
It will take a day for the
paper to dry out.
I wish I had not bought a
pen that writes under water.

A.C. Foster

LONDON E11

A DREAM IN AN ORPHANAGE

A little gate, a garden path, a
bed of flowers, a door opening
wide, two welcoming arms.
A cuddle, brothers and sisters,
laughing.
Watching the telly,
a cat, a dog.
A bedtime story,
a goodnight kiss.
Baked beans for breakfast.
Leaving for school, a wave
from a mum and dad.

B.N. Pople

LONDON SW3

THE
LAST TIME
WE HAD PEANUT
BUTTER . . .

My dad opened the jar
of peanut butter and began
spreading his toast . . .
Simon was violently
sick, Andrew committed
suicide, I ran under a bus,
grandma was hit by a meteorite,
baby Tom ate his rattle and
mother jumped through the
window but my dad carried on
spreading his toast.

Kathryn Wheeler

OUR
FURRY FRIENDS

THE SPACEMAN AND THE DINOSAUR

There was a spaceman
and he met a dinosaur and
they went to the dinosaur's
house and played on the
swings and then they brushed
their teeth.
They went to the pub
and played on the swings
and then they went home
and brushed their teeth
and went to bed.

Alexander Osmond-Brims

CAMBRIDGE

Age 4¾

— 1985 2ND PRIZE – UNDER 18 —

THE MAN, THE WOMAN, AND THE PARROTS

When the woman entered
the tube-train, the
man was there again. The
carriage was full of parrots.
At Baron's Court the man
walked up the empty platform
which waited for the rattle
of a Piccadilly train.
The parrots went as far as
Regent's Park. For the
zoo, she supposed.

Stella Platts

STOCKPORT

A HOMILY FOR AMPHIBIANS – VERONICA THE TOAD FINDS THAT APPEARANCES CAN DECEIVE (ESPECIALLY ONE'S OWN)

Veronica wanted to be a frog.
'A shiny, green skin!'
she gasped, covering her
brown warts in pond slime,
'I *am* a frog!'
Seeing the heron, she wasn't
afraid – a froggy leap could save
her. Sadly, a toad hop did not.
'That frog tasted of toad,'
thought the heron,
'Revolting!'

John Watson

CAMBERLEY

JILL'S SHOPPING ADVENTURE

Once upon a time
there was a hedgehog
called Jill. She was coming
home from the shops but
the food fell out of
her bag. She looked behind
her and she saw her shopping.
Jill went home and sewed
the hole up and then
went back to fetch her
shopping.

Angela Witham

PRESTON

Age 6

THE SHORT LIFE STORY OF A BEE (IN BEE'S LANGUAGE)

Buzz
Buzz buzz
buzz buzz buzz
drone buzz drone
drone buzz drone buzz
drone drone buzz buzz drone
buzz drone drone buzz buzz
buzz drone buzz drone drone
buzz drone drone buzz drone
buzz drone buzz drone
buzz drone buzz
buzz drone.
'Gulp!'
'Yuk!'
'Yeeeouch!' (He got
swallowed by someone.)

Victoria Pilling

DERBY

Age 12

THE DAY I MET A BUDGIE WITH A BENT WING WHO WAS WEARING AN EARRING

I walked into the
budgie cage. He was gobbling
down his delicious breakfast,
a cold and mouldy chip. He
wore a grasshopper's antennae
to keep his wing straight.
He had curlers in his feathers
and eyelashes!!! He put
on his swimming-trunks, called
goodbye and walked off to
the goldfish bowl.

Caroline Dibnah

CAMBRIDGE

Age 11

— *1985 RUNNER UP – UNDER 18* —

THE HOUND'S
DREAM

He was being pursued through
the woods. His pads bled, his
tongue swelled, choking
him. His heart pounded
crazily, as if to burst. They
closed in, ripping his flesh
asunder — a pack of foxes. He
awoke, panting, trembling . . .
ashamed. Then the horn blew,
and an alluring scent
stirred his blood . . .

Susan E. Thorpe

LINCOLN

THE
CIRCUS FREAK
SHOW

'Ladies and Gentlemen,
I will place Dalton on
some coal.'
Dalton blanched.
'Now Dalton on a pillar-box.'
Dalton's jaundiced view
of his patron permeated his
whole being.
'A fig leaf.' Dalton blushed.
'A piece of amber.' Dalton's
envy of the audience's freedom
began to show.
'Dalton, a colour-blind
chameleon.'

D. C. Lee

BARNSLEY

— *1985 RUNNER UP – ADULT* —

ENGLAND'S
LAST DRAGON

The shouts grew louder.
They'd finish him this time.
Old, feeble with loss of blood,
escape was impossible. Wearily,
he rose. Better to face them
proudly than be trapped in
the cave. Cursing the
maiden-snatching ancestor
who had caused his tribe's
extinction, he limped into the
sunlight. And waited.

Daphne Garcia

LONDON SW18

THE COCKSURE CHICKEN

'*I* came first,'
declared the chicken.
Her psychiatrist was very
pleased:
'We have so many cases of
eggomania; pulloprimacy makes
a nice change.'
One night the fox came.
Passing the eggs without a
second glance, he seized the
chicken and made off.
'With me, chickens always
come first,' he said.

Sister Susan Elisabeth

OXFORD

SO PASSES
AN ANCIENT
AND POWERFUL
DYNASTY

I have ruled the world
with strength, dignity for ever.
But now, with darker days, my
strength wanes. If today
brings no blessed warmth
I may not see tomorrow. Then
those little furry creatures will
scuttle unheeded over my bones.
Such creatures are as nothing.
They will never remember
Tyrannosaurus.

Anon.

POST-
CATASTROPHE

THE
POSTCARD

Friendless, he despatched
a letter to the twelfth
century. Illuminated scrolls
arrived by return post.
Jottings to Tutankhamun
secured
hieroglyphs on papyrus;
Hannibal sent
a campaign report.
But when he addressed the
future, hoping for cassettes
crammed with wonders, a
postcard drifted back with
scorched edges. It glowed
all night.

Guy Carter

LONDON W1

— *1985 2ND PRIZE – ADULT* —

58

ANOTHER STORY ON THE THEME OF – AFTER THE HOLOCAUST

Fall-out shelter
built by wealthy businessman
(complete with vault).
– IT HAPPENED –
he and family
went down to safety.
Weeks, months went by
until at last the atmosphere
was safe. Emerging – piles
of rubble stretching in
all directions. A small
voice piped up. 'Are we
still rich though Dad? . . .
DAD . . .!'

B.A. Barnett

GUILDFORD

CONQUERING
HEROES
ALL!

They had worked for
peace, spoken and demonstrated
against weapons and armies.
Initially unpopular, some had
even been imprisoned.
Yet, finally, their Government
had succumbed. Money once
allotted to defence had been
transferred to housing and
education.
What full lives they planned to
live — but that was before the
invasion.

Sheila Cave

LONDON SW1

THE
NIHILIST'S DOUBLE
VISION

He sits at his typewriter. The
world seems too grim to
write about. He lights his tenth
cigarette; the matchhead
jets into his eyeball. Blinded!
He thinks: everything was
okay until a second ago.
Wait . . . Whew, that's better.
Soon he was seeing clearly.
The world looked grim all over
again.

Martin Amis

'MINNIE'
PIT DISASTER
1918

Because the village
was small it was only frantic
minutes before the women,
breathless, gathered at the
pithead. It was months before
the last recoverable body
was reburied. Some lost
father, husband, sons; others,
sanity; wandering, pinafored,
in a limbo of hopeless
expectancy, waiting,
without tears,
for something to bury.

Brian Stanley

NEWCASTLE-UNDER-LYME

ARCHAEOLOGY REBORN

The ruin was so
ancient, even before the
war, that nobody knew
what it was.
After the war, memories
improved.
'Oh that,' local people
said when strangers asked.
'That was a Job Employment
Centre.'
And off they went
to hunt deer or dog.
The World was made over
anew.

Joseph Adcock

W. HARTLEPOOL

WHO
MADE THE
SUN?

Once there was no
sun and four people
were in a war against
twenty others. They
fired beams of light because
it was dark. When it was
war time they went to fight.
They were not good shots.
They shot at the sky together.
It stayed and made
the sun.

Eleanor Sully

YEOVIL

Age 6

ANOTHER STORY
ON THE THEME
OF THE
LAST MAN ON
EARTH

Yes, humanity was dying.
The sun boiled and great
deserts covered the Earth. The
sands moved, and crawled
towards the last town.
The Last Man came out and ran
to the sands, spade and pail
in hand. He began to dig.
It was his sixth birthday.
He built a castle.

Brian Aldiss

— *COMMISSIONED EXAMPLE* —

IF YOU WERE THE ONLY GIRL IN THE WORLD

The neutron bombs had fallen
and killed everyone else.
Somehow she escaped.
The grass was still green.
Flowers still bloomed, the sun
shone. She washed her hair
in the stream,
peeled off her clothes
and lay down – the snake
sidled up to her.
'Psst,' he said
'I have an idea.'

N. Gillies Watson

LOVE

TIME IS A MOTORWAY. IF YOU DON'T LIKE ONE LANE YOU COULD SLIP INTO ANOTHER

The woman wept for the
loss of her man. In a parallel
time the man grieved for the
death of his woman.
She turned and went through
a door she had not known
existed. The man did the same.
In the connecting corridor they
clasped hands.
Together they walked away.

Iris Bishop

TORQUAY

THE COURSE OF
TRUE LOVE
ON THE A233

Tyres scream, smoke
briefly fumes, as brakes
are slammed. Out she flings,
the driver – and so does he.
In single file they stamp up the
leafy road, no word spoken.
She abruptly turns – so
does he.
They return to their seats
in the car, faces stiff,
and roar away.

Vera Hickman

WESTERHAM

THE
ONLY THING
YOU CAN BE
SURE OF
IS THE PAST

He said she had sworn she
didn't mind. She denied it.
He said she changed her mind
to suit her argument;
next time they quarrelled
he secretly recorded the
dispute.
Weeks later, he recalled her
words; she denied them.
He re-played the tape. She
said: 'We have no future
together.'

Peter Whitbread

EAST DEREHAM

AN INVITATION TO CONSIDER THE IMPLICATIONS OF AN ACT OF THOUGHTLESS COMBUSTION

In the primordial soup
a bond forms between two
atoms. Life to be begins.
Alas the link soon breaks.
Atoms are forever.
By miraculous chance these
same atoms are reunited, side
by side, in this paper.
Please keep it!
Do not burn it or they will
be parted for eternity.

David Bremner

DUNDEE

THE SANDS OF TIME – THE SEAS OF ETERNITY

She wandered along the beach.
The waves whispered her name
as he had done before.
They were happy then.
Running along the sand.
Falling into each
other's arms.
Then he had drowned.
She was alone!
But no longer:
Walking out into the sea
she was as one with
him – forever.

Judith Perkins

URMSTON

SO, THE MAGIC DID WORK THEN – WELL, IT ALWAYS IS MAGIC, ISN'T IT?

At the fair, he visited
the old fortune teller. In
the dark tent, she bent her
head, a golden ringlet escaped
from her scarf, or was it her
ear-ring? She predicted love
for him by nightfall. At
the carnival dance, they
met, loved forever. He
and a gold haired
girl.

Pamela Pickton

TEDDINGTON

73

LOVE, ALONE,
NEED NOT
BE LONELY

He died,
after 30 years of marriage.
She, remembering their plans,
moved to a brave new life,
miles away beside the sea.
All seemed idyllic. But
he had not been there. Soon,
loneliness tore her apart.
Sadly she returned to where
he had been. Still alone,
she was not lonely.

Ethel Upchurch

PETERBOROUGH

ALL'S
AT THE FAIR IN
LOVE AND
WAR

I saw them swinging
together, hands clasped, as
the Big Wheel rose.
Steady-handed, hating
his deceit, I won a giant
panda on the Rifle Range.
The Wheel turned; they
descended, laughing.
Later, on the crazy
Wonder-Waltzers of my
mind I let him take
me home. The past
dissolves, like
candyfloss.

Hilary Barton

ULVERSTON

TWO GIRLS COMPARED

I adored her.
Yet I regretted:
her false honesty
her deep-and-meaningful-ness
her grace that scorned my
dumpy form.
her vivacity, flaunting her
promise, bursting bud as
a dewed, velveted briar rose
her complexity
my own remorseful envy and
shallow self.

Sara Pennell

LITTLE
WEAKNESSES

A
PARTICULARLY
POTENT
HOME BREW

Through eyes
surrounded by bruises
she watched the tablets
dissolve. Then she poured
the whisky carefully back into
the bottle.
She had no suspicion
that he would join Alcoholics
Anonymous that day. So a
tramp rooting in the litter-bin,
incredulous at such unexpected
treasure, would die
in his place.

Norman Longmate

RICHMOND

THE
INNER MAN

Their marriage was
a perfect union of trust
and understanding. They
shared everything – except
his desk drawer, which,
through the years remained
locked.
One day, curiosity
overcame her. Prised open,
there was – nothing.
'But why?' she asked,
confused and ashamed.
'I needed a space of my
own', he replied sadly.

Christine M. Banks

A RELIEF
TO ALL
CONCERNED

'I must go. It's very urgent.'
'More important than I am?'
she asked. He left hurriedly.
'I never want to see you
again,' she screamed after him.
A door banged.
'Harry,' she called, 'Come back.'
Silence.
A cistern flushed.
A door opened.
'What the hell's the
matter now?' he said.

Elizabeth Georgiana Bolton

OMBERSLEY

A
CAUTIONARY
TALE FOR
NON-SMOKERS

Henry Mortimer stopped
smoking.
His wife was delighted
and daily pointed out to him
the benefits to his health,
their finances and the
atmosphere.
Unable to tolerate
these reminders of his
abstinence any longer, he
finally throttled her.
He enjoys his smoke at
permitted hours and is a
model prisoner.

Elizabeth Georgiana Bolton

OMBERSLEY

THE
STRIPED
PULLOVER

Bad news.
Another friend gone.
Two in the same week. Both
my age. Both heart attacks.
Who next?
Curse that garrulous
neighbour last Sunday.
'Dreamed you were dead,' she
chattered. 'Recognised your
pullover. Funny, eh?'
For her, maybe. For me,
anguish. Do deaths go
in threes?
I burned that pullover!

Geoffrey Mountain

ACOMB

THE
LURE OF LIFE

A girl sat in her rented
room. She had just, blithely,
painted a picture of
Plato's horses. She lit
a Disque Bleu and decided
to be pretentious no longer.
Light filtered through
the blinds and made shadows
reminiscent of a Cubist
masterpiece. She concluded
that honesty could wait
for another day.

Alexandra Clark

KINGSTON-ON-THAMES

THE STORY
OF A WOMAN
WHO MISTAKENLY
IDENTIFIES HERSELF
AS A GOLDFISH

Antonia's goldfish
swam round and round its
cornerless bowl, looking out
from within.
Meanwhile, Antonia paced
her room, alone, and looked
through windows.
But her room had sharp
corners, which stabbed her
when she fell.
Her room is soft now, and
her mind resents those eyes
looking in from without

Elizabeth White

HORSHAM

Age 17

WAR AND PEACE

HOW TO SURVIVE
BY JUST NOT
TURNING UP

Joe ducked the
history lesson because
the subject bored him, and
his truancy career was launched.
Faced with some unpleasant
prospect he just faded from the
scene like a Bedouin.
The disastrous drop at Arnhem
was effected without Joe who
was absent without leave.
Joe cared little
for historic
occasions.

A. Wilson

MANCHESTER

THE AFFLUENT SOCIETY

The old man
sat alone in the sun;
thinking of Arthur his
friend drowned in the mud
at Flanders, his only son lost
at sea in '42, and watching
the village youths spraying
obscenities on the wall
of the church.
Who is left to die
for freedom? he
thought.

H.O. Phillips

CORBY

FIGHTING
FOR RIGHT

Peace was long ago
and in another country.
These men were his enemies,
he believed. He was fighting
for democracy, for liberty for
all. Like Hell. Levelling his
assault rifle at a conscript
of two weeks' standing
he squeezed out a lethal
burst. Thank Christ
the dead don't
vote.

S.D. Smart

EDINBURGH

'EVEN FROM THE MOST VIOLENT UNIONS, NEW LIFE CAN BE BORN'

All day the
battle raged — with bloody,
agonising screams. Saxon,
Norman, husband, son and
father. The prize — a kingdom.
Now the field is green
and red, and artists paint
the majestic Abbey walls.
Historians propound theories,
write books.
And I write English.
The union consummated, a new
England was born.

S. Wiseman

CIRENCESTER

THE
BEST EVER
NUCLEAR FALL-OUT
SHELTER

London 2020.
Individual nuclear
fall-out shelters were
common. Bob prided himself
on his. 'The best,' he mused,
whilst fishing. 'Beta and
gamma neutralisers,
urine-water convertor,
air purifier . . .'
The siren made him jump.
'My God. It's here. Four
minute warning.'
Then he laughed. He
was five minutes from home.

Dr J.A.F. Carter

CLITHEROE

MIRACLES

COVETED POSSESSIONS

They had more than me.
George had a new bicycle,
polished, sacred almost, no
one could ride it. Sarah had a
dolls house and a dolls pram,
never to be used
by other dolls.
I had a butterfly in a jar.
I let it go.
It set us both free.

A.V. Millichip

STOURBRIDGE

IF ONLY
I COULD RUN

I'm pushed around all
day in my wheelchair. I go
to watch football matches.
If only I could run.
When I'm in my bed I can
look around my room.
I see on my pictures people
running.
But in my sleep. My legs
are strong. I can RUN.

Stephen Moore

LIGHTNING

In youth, Smith
was struck and crippled
by lightning. After years
in a wheelchair, he was weary
of life and planned to end it.
During a thunderstorm, he
wheeled himself under a
tree. The metal and
timber drew the lighting.
He was struck again.
Recovering, he found
he could walk.

M. G. Sherlock

LONDON SW1

EASTER, BLOODY EASTER

Last train home, reading about
the Turin Shroud. Fleetingly,
the windowed reflection of
thorn-crowned Christ
sits opposite. Miraculously,
blood-spots appear on the white
headcloth of the seat.
Tremblingly, he takes it home
to suburbia. Inexorably, the
cloth demands sacrifice,
obedience to Christ,
poverty. Thoughtfully, his
wife launders it . . .

Magnus Magnusson

VARIATIONS ON A THEME OF THE LAST MAN ON EARTH

'The last man on Earth
sat alone. Suddenly there
was a knock on the door . . .'
This cryptic cliché is resolved by
assuming we live in a circular
Universe, spatially and
temporally.
To continue:
'A woman entered. Her name,
like the man's introductory
remark, was palindromic.
He rose.
"Madam, I'm Adam."'

Michael Derry

ILFORD

LIFE'S LITTLE IRONIES

THE PURSUIT OF YOUTH

The blonde and her
young student lover lived
together in his bedsitter.
She regarded the mirror
and worried. With fear in
her heart, she shopped every
lunch-hour, until their
room was stacked with lipsticks,
shoes and dresses.
One evening, opening the
wardrobe, she failed to see
his suit was gone.

Suzi Robinson

LONDON N20

DOUBLE INDEMNITY

Pamela hated her twin:
her mirror-image in appearance,
her opposite in temperament.
Her tempestuous spirit
recoiled from her tepid sibling.
Yet she doubted that she
could live without the sister
to whom she was attached.
Experimentally she drove home
the knife and died.
Siamese twins suffer from
this handicap.

Kay Evans

TAKING TELEVISION TOO SERIOUSLY CAN BE TERRIBLY, TERRIBLY DANGEROUS

A man woke up one night,
disturbed by the sound of
wings flapping. So, being a
television addict, he naturally
assumed it was Dracula, and
died of fright. But it
was really the Angel of Death
in a hurry. 'What a dirty
trick,' he thought, 'but it
did save time.'

Joseph McMahon

BURNTISLAND

HOSPITAL DINNERS

One day Bobby had
just come home from school.
He had school dinners. He
hated them. He decided
to break his leg so
he could go to hospital
and have hospital dinners.
He liked the plan very
much. He broke his leg and
went to hospital.
The dinners were horrid.

Samantha Donoghue

BARNSLEY

Age 8

LEAVING NO CARBON COPIES OF LOVE LETTERS TO AN IMAGINARY GIRL IN AN IMAGINARY ROMANCE

The jilted man
believed his former
lover had sold his love
letters to music publishers.
Each time a new song was aired
the lyrics sounded like his
own. His psychoanalyst
suggested writing letters
to an imaginary girl
as therapy.
These became hits
and the psychoanalyst
disappeared like frost in
summer.

John Docherty

OLD TRAFFORD

IN THE BEST CIRCLES LOVE WILL FIND A WAY TO ENCOMPASS TRIANGLES

By the young Countess's grave her lover bowed his head and wept uncontrollably. For seven years, her ageing husband turning a discreet blind eye, he had shared her favours. The Count laid an encouraging arm across his shoulders. 'Do not despair, my friend. I promise you, I shall marry again.'

Eve Jennings

PEEL

THE STORY
OF A MAN WHO
SOLD HIS LIFE

A writer, growing tired of
selling his emotions, decided
to write one great work,
then leave his profession.
So he sat down at his
desk and wrote of love,
hate, violence, compassion,
in fact of a whole lifetime
of experiences.
The critics applauded it
as the funniest book
they'd ever read.

Alex Allinson

Age 16

THE DARK
FANTASTIC

SOME SPELLS ARE BETTER LEFT UNCAST, THEIR MAGIC WORDS UNSAID

Appealing to my
witching powers, friend
Sarah begged I remove her
husband's bullying boss.
Nightly alone I danced; intoned;
mixed brews; stuck pins.
Later a skidding lorry
killed the boss, his dog,
and our long friendship.
'You *know* I adore
animals,' Sarah wept, 'and
am Chairperson of the
Collie Club.'

M. Field

ST. ALBANS

NOW
LOOK WHAT
YOU'VE DONE

Spoons, scissors, radio
masts, all bent when Celia
was near. It was her
secret – but for how long?
She heard that an
international expert on
psychokinesis was to give a
public lecture in Hull. She *had*
to unburden herself to him.
She crossed the Humber Bridge.
There were no survivors.

Lynn Picknett

LONDON SE5

A
HAPPY ACCIDENT

I roam fantasy lands
on spiralling and dipping
Wings. Sights beyond vision,
sounds beyond hearing,
sensations beyond touch. I
know them all. They are mine.
Each day they search for
some improvement. 'Tragic
accident, brain damage,'
they murmur. 'Keep talking,
bring him back to reality.' But
I am not theirs.

A. Winch

ST. AUSTELL

THE
GOOD FAIRY,
AND
THE TALE OF
HOW SHE CHOSE
ONE TO SPEAK
FOR ALL

'You can have
three wishes,' said the Good
Fairy to Brian. He thought and
thought and thought, then said:
'Peace on earth for evermore.'
'Granted,'
said the Good Fairy.
Brian thought again. 'And
no more disease or death!'
'Granted,'
said the Good Fairy.
'And a chocolate bar!'
Brian was four . . .

R. G. Wheeler

POOLE

WE WENT TO THE CHURCHYARD

'It was very **SPOOKY**,'
Dean cried.
'There's nothing to be afraid
of,' our teacher said.
We saw a big tomb covered
with ivy. The top was broken.
'There's a ghost in there,'
we said.
Dean screamed.
'Nothing can hurt you,'
our teacher said.
She tripped over a gravestone.
We laughed.

Shaun Harris

TOTTENHAM

Age 6½

EVERY NIGHT OUR ANCESTORS SLEPT IN FEAR OF MONSTERS

I read a story to Polly. Evil
chased Good through
forests. Polly's round eyes
were on my lips. Evil closed in,
the child caught her breath.
Then, Good triumphed, Evil
died. I closed the book, she her
eyes, and, thinking into pillows,
murmured, 'Read it to me again
tomorrow . . . tomorrow . . .'

Ian McEwan

— *COMMISSIONED EXAMPLE* —

THE INTERVAL

'Controller, there are
radio signals emanating
from planet Earth.'
'You are certain?'
'We've checked. From
all accounts it is now
their twentieth century.'
'Refresh my memory, when
did we receive the very first
wave of earth transmissions?'
'Some fifteen thousand earth
years ago, sir.'
'I wonder why the long
silence?'

Raymond William Seaton

RUGBY

TELL ME THE STORY OF THE FROG PRINCE AGAIN – PLEASE MOTHER!

Once upon a time,
a beautiful princess met
a tall handsome prince.
They got married and had
three wonderful children.
One day on their anniversary
she kissed him tenderly and
much to her horror he had
turned into an ugly frog.
Screaming, she rushed
straight to the nearest
mirror . . .

B. A. Barnett

GUILDFORD

THE CANNIBAL ARMCHAIR

Once upon a time,
an armchair swallowed me.
Its stomach lining was made of
expensive violet satin.
Its kidneys were made of
black velvet.
I climbed up its ribs and
slid down its backbone.
Halfway down, I tore a hole in
the chair and climbed out.
I was very glad.

Susie Allain

WINCHESTER

Age 11

MAKING
WHOOPEE

MORE THINGS ARE WROUGHT BY PRAYER THAN ARE DREAMED OF

Martha's budgie, Peaches,
kept repeating
'Kiss me, Loverboy,'
shaming Martha when the
vicar called.
Vicar said 'My budgie, Peter,
prays incessantly.
Perhaps piety is infectious.
Bring Peaches to visit.'
The Vicarage budgie was
praying. They opened the cage.
'Kiss me, loverboy,' said
Peaches. 'Hallelujah, my prayers
answered,' said Peter joyfully.

M. G. Holmes

GILLINGHAM

HAMPSTEAD
HEATH
ON BANK HOLIDAY
MONDAY

The fair had hardly
opened when the rain began,
sending the crowds scurrying for
shelter back to cars, under
trees and on the dodgems.
The sun came out just as
suddenly, making a magnificent
coloured arc in the sky.
On the big wheel, I touched
the rainbow with my hand.

Kay Dixon

LONDON

EDEN, AND HOW THE BEGATTING BEGAN

'Look, Evie!'
yelled Adam, experiencing
the very first manifestation.
Eve gawped.
'Does it hurt?' she asked.
His proposition, quite
instinctive, sounded bizarre.
'You must be joking!'
shrieked Eve.
Eventually, she submitted;
thereafter, she enthused.
'You're getting fat,'
remarked Adam, several
weeks later.
'Probably all these damned
apples,' said Eve, uncertainly.

Spencer Smith

DERBY

NIGHT STARVATION

Hungry in the early
hours, he helped himself
to Soave and smoked salmon
from the 'fridge. Refreshed,
he tiptoed upstairs, slipping
silently into bed beside
ravishing, resting Rowena.
Having ravished – and
rested – at 4 a.m. the
burglar departed, stealing
a last kiss, her diamond
jewellery, her furs
and her Ferrari.

Mrs J. Coyte

LIFE IS
A SONG – IF
YOU CAN SING
LIKE A BIRD

Gerald sipped his
drink and looked across
the courtyard. He reflected
on his life.
Young man in a hurry.
Married well. Banker's
daughter.
A pity Vanessa had
grown so fat when he
loved slim girls like
Trudy.
Murder they'd called it.
He threw the cocoa
dregs through the
iron bars –

Harry Walters

LONDON SW14

AN
INTERLUDE AT
THE PARTY

They waited.
Empty glasses were
scattered around the room
and the French windows opened
wide to the warm night air. A
pair of shoes stood on the patio
and a shawl by the pond. The
helicopter skimmed the
trees northwards.
She would just make the
off-licence before
closing time.

John H. Drew

KENILWORTH

THE
COMPULSIVE
GAMBLER

Fify thousand pounds
rested upon the final
card. The seven of clubs,
not enough. He paid up with
a wry smile, walked out to his
Lotus and roared away.
Another car slowed him down.
Should he overtake, they were
approaching a bad bend.
He overtook.
It was not his night.

G. Kennell

NUNEATON

LIFE AND TIMES

THE RIGHT AND WRONG WAYS TO REGARD MATERIAL POSSESSIONS

Chapter One

They stood looking at the dazzling object, mesmerised, until their eyes fell out. Panic took control, they turned and blindly ran over the cliff edge.

Chapter two

The boy, his back to the spectacle, used the light it shed to guide him past the cliff, to the safety of his chosen destination.

The end

Anna Chilvers

NUNEATON

Age 15

— *1982 1ST PRIZE – UNDER 18* —

AT NOON

I had been bothered
with phone calls before
but none really frightening.
The phone rang, I picked it
up and a man's voice said,
'Time stops at noon.'
I was worried and decided to
go down town. I returned
at noon and entered the
room, entered the
room, entered the . . .

Stuart Calder

DUNDEE

CAREER PROSPECTS

Nice chap, our new
headmaster. Keen to make
changes. He 'welcomed' our
suggestions. Never adopted one.
Had his own ideas – for
'maximising motivation',
'individualizing discipline',
'neutralising competition',
and so on.
Absolute chaos. But he never
saw it like that. He's a Director
of Education now.
Good with words, you see.

Berwick Coates

BARNSTAPLE

UPSIDE DOWN
IN A FIRE DRILL

It was Blogend school,
(My school fire drill).
Mr Fenwick (headmaster)
found me up-side down in a
rubbish bin, waving my feet
like a helicopter, about to
take off.
'What are you doing?' asked
Mr. Fenwick.
'Panicking, sir!' I answered
He suddenly turned as red
as a beetroot.
'Trust you!'

Andrew Watts

DEVIZES

Age 10

AT LAST, UNABRIDGED, THE FULL STORY OF SOLOMON GRUNDY, TOLD BY HIMSELF

Tuesday – Wetness my earliest
Recollection, and a Voice
pronouncing my Name.
Wednesday – After a Whirlwind
Courtship, my Dearest and I
plighted our Troth to Eternity.
Friday – My Dearest is with
Child! So many Plans, but the
Ague hath Hold of me Still.
I shall deal with them
after the Weekend.

(Note: the original, truly mini
saga on which this bloated
and prolix version draws runs
to just 32 words.)

Nick Alexander

KIRKNEWTON

128

THE INVOLUNTARY VOYAGE AND TRAGIC EMULSIFICATION OF AN EDWARDIAN COUNTRY WOMAN

Thread-thin Miss Pym slid
down the plughole and
her bathwater swept her into the
sea. She floated past Europe.
Japanese pearl-divers panicked
and breathed in. A whale
swallowed her and she became
margarine in Archangel.
Her slender friend Agnes
mourns, and baths with
a coathanger between her
teeth.

Frank Muir

— *COMMISSIONED EXAMPLE* —

THE SKINHEAD'S ASIAN VICTIM WAS THE MAN WHO SAVED HIS LIFE

The scalpel blade
is poised. Deftly the
surgeon makes the first incision.
Soon the inflamed appendix
is removed.
The boy feels no more pain.
Five years later, the knife is
poised. The boy laughs as
the blade enters the victim's
heart. Another dead paki.
The doctor feels
no more pain.

P. Morris

LONDON N4

A STORY OF TRIBULATION WITH A MODERN FAIRY-TALE ENDING

He was reported missing,
believed dead. His wife
grieved and the years passed.
Then following a tip from a
friend, she found him living in
Valparaiso with a rich woman
who had helped him escape
from a prison-camp.
She divorced him and lived
happily ever after, on
the alimony.

John Sylvester

YARMOUTH

FULFILMENT
FOR ALL
CONCERNED.
OR
UNCONCERNED?

The faraway, romantic
places called to her. But,
happy again at Bournemouth,
'Rolling stones,' he never
failed to say, 'gather no moss.'
At last he died, and, having
bought herself a cruise around
the world, she ordered the
inscription for his
tombstone.
'Rest in Peace', it said,
'And gather moss'.

Geraldine Cox

LONDON SE9

ACCEPTANCE, ACCEPTANCE AND ACCEPTANCE

Accepting the post, she became the backbone of the firm. For thirty years she supervised underlings and junior management impartially and firmly, bowing to the Supremo alone. Accepted by all, she arrived early, finished late. Unappreciated by a new hierarchy, she offered her resignation which, to her horror, was accepted.

K. G. Gordon

CONGLETON

50 WORDS ON THE STABLE AND WELL-BALANCED LIFE OF MR AVERAGE

He was born.
He attended school
at five years old. For
several years he believed
that the heads of mature
dandelions were fairies. He
took piano lessons. He married
and washed his foreign car
every Sunday. After three
score and ten years he
died, but only his
wife noticed.

Anstey R. Baker

KENT

Age 16

134

THE
OLD AND TIRED
MINER

He put on his dirty cap,
and an old black coat, picked
up his pick and walked down
the yard,
opened the rotting
wooden gate and stepped into
the dirty backs. In the
distance he saw the
pit where he worked. Down
Pearce Lane he walked, not
a bit excited.

Caroline Lowe

LEIGH

Age 10

SOME IN RAGS, SOME IN JAGS, AND ONE IN A VELVET GOWN

Exchanging the tiara for
a small cloth cap, she slipped
away, leaving the rich palace
laughter behind her.
The final chords echoed through
the maze of concrete passages as
the last train trundled away,
and she smiled happily at
the mound of coins in the violin
case at her feet.

Claire French

COLCHESTER

Age 15

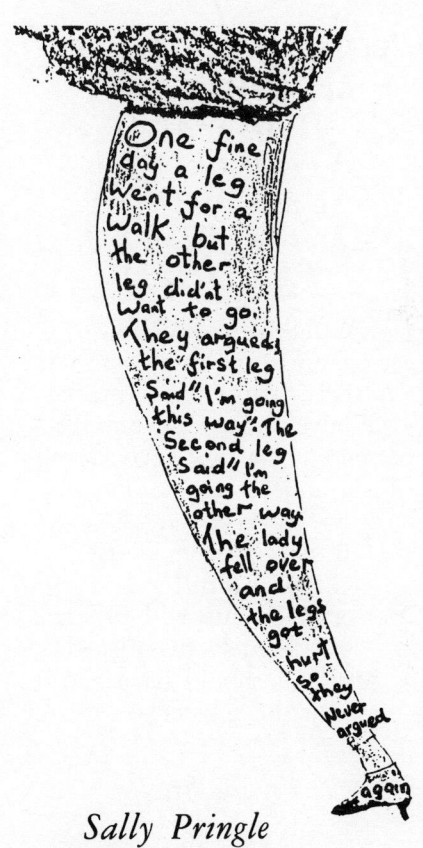

One fine day a leg went for a walk but the other leg did'nt want to go. They argued, the first leg said "I'm going this way". The second leg said "I'm going the other way. The lady fell over and the legs got hurt so they never argued again

Sally Pringle
THORPE MANDEVILLE
Age 8

— *1985 RUNNER UP – UNDER 18* —

137

I
SHOE-HORNED ON MY DESIGNER JEANS AND STROLLED IN SEARCH OF A LITTLE BISTRO, FAMISHED

A pinkly plump prawn
peered up from white porcelain.
'A trifle Spartan,' I ventured.
'Nouvelle Cuisine. Simply
presented, classically conceived.
Taste and texture unimpaired
by sauce or garnish.'
I devoured every morsel.
'The Bill?'
'An open cheque will be fine.'
I left, vaguely dissatisfied.
Maybe I should have had
the lobster?

Frank Steel

Age 16

ANCIENT
WORLDS

END
OF THE LINE

It was just one
more beautiful book to
add to the score already
made. Brother Albrecht was
well content.
With a final flourish he
laid down his quill, raising
his head to meet the eyes
of the Abbot and a stranger.
The Abbot spoke: 'Brother
Albrecht, please meet
Johann Gutenberg.'

Eric Ferguson

DORKING

A
HAPPENING
FROM THE
PAST

Sitting alone in the sun-warmed
heather. An approaching noise
of hooves and jingle on
the unseen road. A feeling of
presence – and they passed.
Checked, and there had
been no horses anywhere near
that day. Concluded it was
ghosts of English or Scottish
Cavalry 1745.

H.R.H.

*The Princess
Margaret*

THE
ASCENT OF MAN
(AND THE
ASCENDANCY OF
WOMAN)

When Ugg the Frantic
commanded fire from the
mountain, the earth trembled;
liquid rock spurted.
'Hardly convenient for domestic
heating,' sneered Mrs Ugg.
'Alright!' shouted Ugg, 'so you
got a split-level cave!'
'. . . and I need something
to wheel the baby in.'
'Wheel?' fretted Ugg,
eyeing the full moon,
'wheel . . ?'

Don Wells

ABERDEEN

THERE'S JUST NO PLEASING SOME PEOPLE

The Emperor had
tried seven wives for
a male child but none of
them had produced one for
him so he had them all killed.
His eighth produced a boy.
'Ah,' he said, 'I cannot make
male babies so this cannot
be mine, O Unfaithful One.'
He slew them both.

John Sylvester

GT. YARMOUTH

OUR OUTWARDNESS ANNOUNCED THE SINGLE INWARDNESS WE SHARED

'What is that
you are making?' I asked.
'A new robe for the goddess
of love,' replied the seamstress.
'A *black* robe?' I said.
'Surely she wears white?'
'Not invariably,' she replied.
'This is another order from her
sister the goddess of death.
They love giving presents
to each other.'

Kenneth T. Dutfield

MINCHINHAMPTON

A SUCCINCT HISTORY OF THE ROMAN EMPIRE

The Romans came from
Troy, and conquered the
Latins, Etruscans, Volscii,
Aequi, Veii, Samnites, Pyrrhus
of Epirus, Carthaginians,
Sicilians, Greeks, Syrians,
Spanish, Teutoni, Cimbri,
Syrians (again), Bithynians,
Armenians, Albani, Iberi, the
poor old Syrians again,
the Egyptians, Jews, Gauls,
Parthians, Cantabri, Ethiopians
and Britons, but were beaten
by the Goths.

Laurie Wedd

TONBRIDGE

— 1985 RUNNER UP – ADULT —

***THE
GREATEST SAGA
OF ALL TIME
(SOON TO BE A
MULTI-MILLION
DOLLAR MOTION
PICTURE)
HERE MINI-MISED
INTO
FIFTY WORDS***

Odysseus was a
cunning, resourceful
man who fought with the
Greeks against Troy. Sailing
back from the war, he and his
crew met with a number of
menaces – such as Circe,
the witch who turned men
into pigs – and
overcame them.
But it took him ten
years to get home.

C. C. Shackleton

OXFORD

HOW TO
GET A JOB
AFTER TWO YEARS
ON THE DOLE

To get a mechanic's
job in the factory, Tom
must join the Union.
But the Union refused him
as he was not already working
as a mechanic.
Frustrated, seeking publicity
he fired blank shots at
the Queen.
Tom is now fully employed
for ten years, counting remission
for good conduct.

Don Featherstone

ROMSEY

MACBETH SHOWS A GUEST ROUND HIS GARDEN

'Och, if only I'd more
time for ma hobbies,' sighed
Macbeth as we walked round
the garden at Dunsinane.
He stopped to hose the blood
from his wellies.
'Look,' he said miserably
and thrust a crimson
finger towards the
yellowing plants:
'Tomato, tomato
and tomato, grapes and the
petit pois . . .'

Kevin Swift

RIPON

148

PROSE PRÉCIS: PAINS UP WITH WHICH PRINCE, POTENTLY-POISONED, COULDN'T PUT

My father brought me up
well. My mother played him
who brought me up well false.
My uncle knocked her, then
him off. At his ghost's bidding
I did the man
who knocked the woman
who played the king
who brought me up
well false off in.
Silence, the rest . . .

Chris Nash

WORCESTER

AN
INNOCENT
IN
BABYLON

The villager knew
nothing of the big city.
A little prostitute took him in,
and thought him stupid.
She undressed completely,
complaining of the heat.
Still he made no move.
Back home, telling the story,
he sighed, 'If I'd played my
cards right, I bet I could
have had her . . .'

Vedris Poppat

EAST EALING

'AND ANOTHER THING: HOW DO YOU EXPLAIN ST. MICHAEL'S HOLY NAME EMBLAZONED ON YOUR UNDERGARMENTS?'

It must have been a time-slip.
About 560 years, backwards.
1425.
I knew quite a lot about that
period. I'd been studying
French History on television.
'What's television, Joan?'
they asked.
I tried to explain; living
pictures, voices, music, coming
from the air.
They're just setting light
to the faggots.

David J. Brazier

BEMBRIDGE

— *1985 RUNNER UP – ADULT* —

151

ON LISTENING
TO GREGORIAN
CHANT

The hooded, brown robed
figures file slowly past the
window. I think they probably
smell of old books, goose grease
and sweat.
They begin to sing
and their strange, solemn
music propels their faith across
a thousand years. Perplexed,
unsure, I wonder if my
own disbelief will
last that long.

G. M. Harrison

CLEETHORPES

CRIME AND PUNISHMENT

WATSON'S FATAL BLUNDER, OR, PROFESSOR MORIARTY RETURNS FROM REICHENBACH BUT IS OUTFACED BY SHERLOCK HOLMES

I killed Moriarty when
he attacked my disguised friend.
'Congratulations, Watson,'
sneered the survivor.
Moriarty's voice! He was
disguised as myself! I groaned:
'Moriarty?'
'Correct, Watson. You've
killed Holmes, who
impersonated me.'
'Wrong!' I removed my
disguise.
Moriarty reeled. 'YOU!'
'Elementary, Professor. Poor
Watson – I meant him to
impersonate *me*.'

James Cawthorn

COMEUPPANCE: A STRANGE TALE OF DEATH IN THE DUKERIES

Lord Stentor's butler,
elderly, pink cheeked, saintly
Fred Dunnit, was known as
'Hugh' because milord always
summoned him by rudely
bellowing: 'Hi you!'
When milord was found shot
dead it was pronounced suicide
because he was all alone
in the house. Except of course,
for his servant . . .
The butler Dunnit.

Frank Muir

CHICAGA SAGA

He married the Godfather's
daughter,
Who drank – but never water –
And both their sons
Soon carried guns
And went into bricks and
mortar.

Two crooks in real estate –
Each with a drunken mate –
They both were shot
By a rival lot
Because some rent was late.
Then went
Into cement.

R. S. Philpott

ORPINGTON

CRIME
IN THE CITY

They negotiated in the
limousine. Neat, dark business
suits. Professional men.
The radio news carried another
mugging: pensioner savaged
in Brixton. 'Disgusting,' said
one; 'no law and order any
more.' The other memorised the
photograph of the contract,
a welsher. 'Tell the client,
24 hours and it's done.'
Professional men.

Frederick Forsyth

THE HAUNTED COTTAGE

The villagers envied
the newcomer who could afford
the coveted cottage.
'Of course, you know it's
haunted,' they daily, yearly,
warned her.
Unaccepted in the village,
she looked harassed, her eyes
grew wild. When she hanged
herself, one of them got the
cottage cheaply. And found she
was still there . . .

Pamela Pickton

TEDDINGTON

PROMETHEUS REVISITED – OR THE 'ATLAS SWITCH'

Prometheus was chained to
Mount Caucausus. Daily
an eagle came to eat his liver,
which grew again at night.
An Official climbed up and said
he hadn't paid Income Tax for
2,000 years. Prometheus said
'You try it.' The Official
swapped places. Prometheus
escaped, amid a flurry
of feathers.

Reggie Bosanquet

BOYS
WILL BE BOYS

She saw him in the
garden, shooting at the sparrows
and starlings. 'Jimmy, what
are you doing?' she called,
horrified. 'Come in at once!'
An obedient son to the
last, he came.
'What will the neighbours
think?' she demanded,
not seeing the malevolent
glee in his eyes.
'What neighbours, mother?'

A. Watson

NEWCASTLE-UPON-TYNE

THE
LAST DAY

The prisoner awoke.
He smiled. Today was the
last day. Today they would
let him out.
The prisoner waited.
The keeper opened the door
of the cell. He gave the
prisoner a drink, to celebrate,
he said.
The prisoner slept.
The prisoner awoke. He smiled.
Today was the last day . . .

Allan K. Evans

HARLOW

Age 15

A LIGHT-HEARTED APPROACH AT SOLVING A MYSTERY BY AN INEXPERIENCED YET CLEVER DETECTIVE

A pretty young girl was
ruthlessly murdered as she
lay in bed in a large mansion.
Peter meticulously checked over
the rooms, hunting clues.
Four hours later he returned
to the anxious family.
'The butler did it.'
'But how do you know?'
they all asked.
'It's the logical English
solution!'

Marcus Beard

NORWICH

Age 13

A SATISFIED CUSTOMER

Gordon's memory of
Prewitt thrashing him never
disappeared: the prefect's
study, stifled weeping
and humiliation.
Many years afterwards, a
cloudburst drove him into a
shoe shop. Unrecognised
himself, he knew Prewitt
immediately. Countless pairs
of shoes later, Gordon
sauntered away without buying
any, leaving Prewitt kneeling
in shaming, leathery
chaos.

Joanna Lumley

POSSESSED
BY LOVE

Paulo loved his beautiful wife,
yet they quarrelled violently.
To see her flirting with
other men drove him mad. One
day, he caught her with a
neighbour. 'My life is my own,'
she cried – but Paulo killed her.
He could not distinguish
beween what was proper and
what was property.

Brian Aldiss

ORDINARY
FOLK

AN
EXILE
TRIES TO
WRITE
A MINI-SAGA

Wolverhampton in the winter.
Frost on the railway lines. It's
so drab. Sometimes I long for
the tropics where
I came from.
The sun at zenith every day.
The pleasures of open-air
restaurants every
evening.
But there's work in
Wolverhampton.
You expect all my feelings
in fifty words?

V. V. Fisher

LEWISHAM

WHY
SHOULD IT BE?
HINDU
EPILOGUE

Roddy and I were chota
sahibs together. He, poor
chap, was in trade.
Years later I heard of his
fame as diamond merchant,
Sheriff, Chairman of the Club,
Member of the Assembly.
How I envied him.
Then came news of his
suicide. Envy also died.
Now I can only wonder.

P.V. Wells

WEST HORSLEY

THE WOODLANDERS: CONSEQUENCES, OR, AN EVERYDAY STORY OF HARDY FOLK

Tess of the d'Urbervilles met Jude the Obscure Under the Greenwood Tree, Far from the Madding Crowd. She said to him: 'Seek The Hand of Ethelberta.' He said to her: 'I'm A Changed Man.' The consequence: The Return of the Native, The Mayor of Casterbridge!
The world said:
'Desperate Remedies.'

Margaret Manson

OXFORD

AGONY
COLUMN

Sarah was thirty-four.
Her fashion magazine life
was the envy of her married
friends. She had a red leather
briefcase and a sportscar.
Sarah knew she was happy.
She did not mind men leaving
before dawn. She quite
understood their married
lives.
Her magazine told her
this was normal.

Paul Cuerden

POWICK

I THINK MY DAD MUST BE SUPERMAN

My dad always acts like
Superman. One day we went
for a walk. We saw a man
going to throw himself
off a block of flats. Dad
then flew up and brought the
man down safely. I stood
there absolutely amazed.
My dad came back and
we carried on walking.

Nigel Wyllie

Age 10

THE ANTICS
OF TRIVIALITIES
ON A
WARM SUMMER'S
DAY

It was warm outside;
all the ants were sitting
on deck chairs wearing
sun hats.
It was warm inside:
the dry martinis were
sending up smoke signals.
The room was flooded with
sunlight.
Reflections from the mirror
shimmered on the wall.
Bright colours, but then
a cloud.
No more reflections.

Stephen J. Horner

Age 12

THE HERO
OF THE
MINUTE

The midget's life had
been brief.
'We will commission a mini
saga on him.' The fat publisher
told the little widow.
'No. He was a "big" man.
A large tome or nothing.' She
replied at length fingering
the tiny phial of ash in
her pocket.
'He will be long remembered.'

Angela Colman

KINGSTON-UPON-THAMES

THE AGE OF
TECHNOLOGY

IN THE NAME
OF PROGRESS

The beautiful village was
dying. 'There is no
industry', complained its
inhabitants, 'our young people
are leaving'. The developers
moved in; factories belched
out gas and motorways ate
into the hedgerows. 'They
have destroyed the beauty. We
must escape to the unspoiled
countryside,' cried the
new community — and
moved away.

Maureen Roberts

BOURNEMOUTH

174

WHO
TRAINS WHOM?

He ran happily through
the maze, keeping the red
signs on the right, and
the white signs on the left.
At the end he stopped and
waited until the blue
light came on. Then he
pressed the lever down. The
trap door opened and a
perfectly conditioned
psychologist handed the rat
a piece of cheese.

R. G. Sheldon

WILLINGDON

PROPHETEX

'Electronic Prophet!' scoffed
Jones. 'Rubbish!'
'Try it,' replied Brown, 'but
take care what you ask.'
'Shall I be wealthy?'
asked Jones.
'Affirmative,'
replied Prophetex.
'Shall I live long?'
'Affirmative.'
'Shall I have serious illnesses?'
'Negative.'
'What will win the Derby?'
'Archimedes.'
'Well, I'm damned!' he
gasped admiringly.
'Affirmative,'
said Prophetex.

J. O. Woon

SWINDON

THE EIGHTH NIGHT

That phone. Every night for a week. Nobody speaks, just silence. And now it is past three and I am sweating. Two years ago to the day the man who occupied this office before me died of exposure to radioactivity. Moonlight floods the reactor. Why doesn't the damned thing ring?

Hammond Innes

— COMMISSIONED EXAMPLE —

MILLS AND BOON DISCOVER THE MINI-SAGA OR LOVE AMONG THE LAUNDRY

When Sally found a man's
striped sock curled among
her clothes at the launderette
she returned it to the tall
dark young man with a
shy smile.
They met there every
week for several months,
then were seen no more.
One of their wedding presents
had been a washing machine.

Molly Burnett

ASHFORD

A FABLE

A wealthy scientist on
the frontiers of research
considered passing a
camel through the eye of
a needle. He extracted the
camel's DNA code and
developed a very, very small
form of camel that easily
fitted through the gap.
Unfortunately he mislaid
the camel before he could
get to heaven.

James Atkins

KIRKBY LONSDALE

Age 17

THE GADGET THAT WAS GOING TO BENEFIT THE WORLD AND BRING RICHES TO PAUL

Paul had devoted many years to perfecting an intricate high precision device. His family made financial sacrifices believing that the unique invention would make them all rich. Paul finally proceeded to mass produce the world's first clockwork operated pocket adding machine.

The liquidators used electronic calculators to count the stock.

E. Fleming

LONDON SW6

DAYS OF OUR YOUTH

UNPROMISING PUPIL

The tutor sighed. 'I can't
teach you. Your performance
is mediocre, and your written
work worse. You are a dreamer,
boy; you will never come to
anything, I fear. Here is
a note for your father.'
Trembling, young Ludwig
went home to face the drunken
wrath of the elder
Beethoven.

J. O. Woon

SWINDON

YOU HAVE
TO LIVE NEAR
THE GROUND

A small boy, with all
the time there was, hunted
for snails in the dry
stone walls.
Shells bright as jockey caps;
he set them racing – mocking
their slow sad motions.
Last night, as he
half-dozed in his deckchair,
a gold snail raced past
and plunged mocking
behind the hill.

Laurie Lee

— *COMMISSIONED EXAMPLE* —

OOM BAM BOOBY – THE THIRD YOUNGEST DAUGHTER OF MR & MRS RUSHBOURNE'S NINE DAUGHTERS

Oom Bam Booby was born
in the sixties.
Her parents, university
graduates of dialect and speech
were much in awe of the
tribal inspired pop rhythm
words such as Oom Bam
Booby and Doobee Doobee.
She never forgave her
parents' progressiveness,
and changed her name by
deed poll to Tracy.

Caroline Forbes

LONDON SW8

NOW WE ARE SIX, AND SNIFFING GLUE . . .

Cut from a forest oak
centuries ago, the child's
chair had sat before
the hearth.
The dreaming throne,
in turn, for infant Regency
bucks, Victorian generals and
golden youths doomed to
Flanders mud.
Empty now, displayed in
the Bond Street window;
too precious for use,
too fragile for our
darlings.

Charles Lodge

LONDON SW3

BIRTH
OF EMOTIONS

The mother gazed
lovingly at her newborn
child; father and firstborn
stood watching.
Feelings of protective
tenderness engulfed the
father. The firstborn, puzzled
by stirrings he had never
before experienced and could
not name, did not hear
when his father asked, 'Shall
we call him Abel?'
Cain made no reply.

Joan Wedge

SOUTHAMPTON

A DAY IN THE DEATH OF AN ETHIOPIAN CHILD

The small boy snatched the
biscuit being held out to him.
It was all he ate that day.
He slept, hungry again.
Next day he ate nothing.
That night, he sipped a
dribble of milk, curled up,
and for the first time,
he was full up.
He never woke up!

Colin Evans

LONDON SE9

Age 16

THE LEVELS OF IMPORTANCE AT DIFFERENT AGES OF LIFE

The flood water rose ever
higher, up to their knees
although upstairs.
'I want the boat!' the little
boy screamed – the water
around
his waist.
'It's coming!' the mother
comforted, holding his hand
tightly.
Finally, he wrenched free
and dashed away.
He returned, triumphant,
trailing his sailing
boat behind him.

Sylvia Still

LANCING

A TRIP
TO THE BIG
WET ONE

Forced from the car,
I dread the big wet one.
Approaching her door, my mind
is frozen with dread. The
door opens. A flesh mountain
in an oversize dress towers
before me. I am lifted off
my feet and face the rubbery
lips. It comes . . . the
big wet one . . . smack!

Matthew Ember

WEMBLEY PARK

Age 10

HARRY'S REVENGE: A MORAL TALE

'Pretty Mama!' exclaimed
little Harry. 'When you die
I shall have you stuffed
and keep you.'
But Mama decamped with a
rich industrialist.
Papa barely noticed. Harry,
abandoning his enthusiasm for
taxidermy, embarked on a
lucrative career robbing
elderly women.
His final victim was
Mama — less pretty and
decidedly unstuffed.

Sylvia van Gelder

LONDON N12

LEARNING CONTINUES ONLY BY STRETCHING IT

At five he bounded into
school. He passed examinations
superbly. University
scholarship led to a first
class honours degree.
All success. As a professor,
he realized how much he
didn't know. He gave
his six year old grandson
a piece of elastic.
'Keep it to remind you
to stretch knowledge.'

Frances Bruce

CRANLEIGH

THE HAPPIEST DAYS . . .

At first, school was
fun, but gradually I became
ensnared in its tedious
regularity. More and more
I longed to be free, to
shape my own destiny.
Complaining, I worked hard
to gain success in my
exams.
But now a single week
of school remains . . .
I wish it were longer . . .

Kim Bell

BRISTOL

Age 18

BIG
HEROES – SMALL
BEGINNINGS

Alien beings have
invaded earth!
They look like humans,
but underneath are really
purple, one eyed, with poisoned
fangs, oozing slime and
hissing. It's me against
them all – me, Flash
Gordon, saviour of
the universe. But I HAVE
to save the world . . .
Oh, alright, but leave the
night light on, mum.

Susan E. Thorpe

LINCOLN

THIS IS THE STORY OF MY JOURNEY WHEN I RAN AWAY FROM HOME TO WALES

I ran away a week
after my birthday because I
was sick of everyone
moaning at me. I had some
Hovis and two cans of
soup.
I was ten miles away
from Wales and it was
raining. I ate my 'Heinz
soup' which reminded me
of Grandad and I returned
home.

A. Podam

TWILIGHT
YEARS

RETIREMENT
HOBBIES
FOR
OCTOGENARIANS

Grandfather was eccentric.
Ensconced in the garden shed
for weeks fiddling with
wires and things. 'I will
show you!' he would say.
We humoured him, dear
old chap.
Yesterday the shed and
grandfather vanished. No
noise, smoke or light – just
not there.
He said to expect him back
next week.

M. R. Campbell

NEWBURY

AND WHAT, YOU MAY ASK, DO PEOPLE REALLY KNOW OF YOU?

In the thirties he worked
for a firm in Peru but, in truth,
he was idle, drunk and the
loose ladies' best customer.
Today he is retired, rich
and the essence of Croydon's
respectability. But on
summer nights the glint in
his eye recalls the
glories of his misspent
youth.

E.W. Smithson

CROYDON

WHILE THERE'S LIFE

The conference throbbed
with expectancy.
Dr. Hugo's lecture promised
thrilling revelations
from a lifetime's secret
research into human
rejuvenation.
The octogenarian physician
bounded on stage looking the
epitome of youth.
'My friends,' he began and
collapsed, dead, before them.
Some delegates were
inconsolable. Some mourned
a colleague. Most
mourned hope.

M. A. Cufflin

SIDCUP

198

THE BLIND OLD LADY

They spoke loudly
and slowly to her, as if
her ears and brain were worn
out too. Guiding her here
and there, moving this
and fetching that. Being
there – but always just out
of reach, lest she cling
to them, lest she needed more
than duty . . . lest she
needed love.

Susan E. Thorpe

LINCOLN

199

NEMESIS

They watched the old man
collect his pension, followed
him like twin hawks, closed on
him with practised skill.
Startled, the victim
fell clutching his attackers
who found themselves stumbling
backwards off the pavement
into heavy traffic.
The Coroner said 'Accidental
Death.' The old man, once a
Commando, knew better.

John Johns

LITTLEHAMPTON

A
MOMENT'S
REFLECTION

George stopped dead
A black car sped towards him.
It didn't stop; it didn't see him.
What to do? George never
could move very fast; no need
to since Milly died.
The car hurtled towards him.
Why make the effort?
Brakes screeched . . .
Wonder where she is now?
George stopped, dead.

David Taylor

VIRGINIA WATER

Age 15

— *1985 RUNNER UP – UNDER 18* —

IF GOD INTENDED MOTHERS TO BE MOTORISED HE WOULD HAVE MADE PRIVET HEDGES STRONGER

Don't let mother buy a moped.
We had to catch her as
she went screaming past on
her bicycle.
She never mastered the
art of dismounting and our
hedge has never recovered.
We have already booked
the village institute for
her seventieth birthday,
and I bought a new hat.

Joanne Simms

STOCKPORT

OUR DEAR OLD
GRANNY RETURNS

So sweet she looks, but nervous.
'Lovely to have you back
from . . . that place,
granny dear.'
She smiles.
'How's my dear little
grand-daughter?'
Granny's alone in her room
again. Slyly she starts to grow
claws.
Grand-daughter knocks.
'Come in, pet, all alone?'
'Yes granny.'
'Oh, good . . .' Saliva drips
as door opens.

A. E. Fitch

LIVERPOOL

'DAMN,'
SAID LITTLE
OLD MISS EMILY'S
HOST CHEERFULLY,
'IT'S ALWAYS
BREAKING DOWN'

. . . the holiday cine
crunched . . . stopped . . .
Then Miss Emily saw herself
speeding backwards, summer
cliffs . . . matronly
now, on Harry's arm . . .
Young girl, river, flowery-print
dress . . . little girl
grasping doll . . . bonneted
baby in pram . . .
Miss Emily began to feel
distinctly uneasy.
In the darkened room no one
noticed her sudden stillness.

Jan Godfrey

FAR COUNTRIES

DIFFERENT VALUES, OR WHO GOT THE BEST OF THE BARGAIN?

Harris boasts he gave an
African a cheap watch
for an uncut diamond.
Sold it and gambled the
proceeds for more.

Abukali tells of the tiktik he
swapped for a wife
and two goats.
Harris chases further millions.
Abukali sleeps in the shade
while his children tend
his twenty goats.

R. S. Ferm

THETFORD

— *1985 1ST PRIZE – ADULT* —

206

MEN WHO LIVE IN MUD HOUSES . . .

How the tribe laughed
when the anthropologist
couldn't recognize his own
camel among their herd,
even reminding him
of it as they
waved goodbye.
And when he returned, how
the tribe greeted him
and delighted in telling
him the story of the white
man who couldn't recognize
his own camel . . .

Jonathan Hall

LONDON NW6

BURIAL AT SEA

When we bury
Aboud Abdullah
the moon is a big orange,
levitating itself over Aden.
The ship's engine has stopped.
There is a disorienting
stillness.
Intercom: 'Stern!' – 'Right' –
pause –
Don't damage the propeller.'
Splash.
The Captain mops his mouth.
'Delicious this fish.'
'Must have dined on
Abdullah.'
The Captain vomits.

G.C. Pavledis

LONDON E17
.

TWO SIDES
TO EVERY STORY

'Well, what are you going
to do about it?' he roared.
'I told you he conned his way
into my home, stole from
me and then assaulted me when
I chased him. I've just
spent three months in traction.'
The policeman sighed, 'What's
his name Sir?'
'Jack'
replied the giant.

T. K. Dawber

BLACKBURN

THE DEATH AND RESURRECTION OF A BORINGLY CONSTRICTED PARTNERSHIP

Desiree's fertility dance
faltered . . . her snake had
fainted. Should she abandon
her act and breathe life into
the wobbling head?
No! The show must go on.
Desiree knotted and unknotted
the faccid python over strategic
areas to prolonged male
applause . . . and wondered
if taxidermists stuffed
snakes by metres or yards.

G. W. Tiplady

STOCKPORT

POLITICS

ROD:
REFLECTIONS ON
THE WISDOM
OF NUCLEAR
ARMAMENT

The zoologist kept a caged
male gorilla. Rod became
dangerously morose, and finally
a psycho-analyst was called.
The zoologist found he had
given Rod a loaded revolver.
In horror, he ran after
the man.
'Rod feels threatened. The
gun reassures him.'
'But only a madman would
arm a killer ape!'

Nancy C. Stainer

MILTON KEYNES

WHEN THE POLITICAL PEDLARS OF COCKAIGNE TAKE OVER – THE GOODS AND THE GOODIES VANISH OVERNIGHT

Our Leader promised
houses thatched with pancakes,
pig puddings for bell ropes,
walls built with penny
loaves, Little pigs with
knives and forks sticking
in them, shouting 'Who
will eat me!' and PEACE.
Now houses,
loaves,
pancakes,
and pigs
are all black market.
And it's 'Long Live The
Armed Struggle!'

Ellis Glover

BRIDESTOWE

FRUIT OF
AN OLD TREE

The Chinese
economic delegation left
Heathrow. Sighing, the Foreign
Minister commented, 'Hard
bargainers . . .'
'With something of Old China
about them,' said the P.M.
As they were driven through
gathering autumn mists,
the P.M. said, 'At Chequers,
I saw their chairman stoop
and tuck a fallen leaf
into his empty wallet.'

Nancy C. Stainer

MILTON KEYNES

A SINISTER SAGA

This morning my left
hand mutinied. It waggled
furiously in semaphore:
'I'm fed up with being
neglected, stuffed into pockets
with loose change and
forever playing Horatio to
that right hand's Hamlet!
I'm pushing off!'
Ashamed, I consented to
amputation. It scuttled off, an
independent fist, plotting an
ambidextrous republic.

Guy Carter

LONDON W1

— *1985 RUNNER UP – ADULT* —

ME AND OUR
MAGGIE

Will the Prime Minister
explain why she allowed rain
on Bank Holiday and why
she forgot my birthday.
It's always the same,
she gets all the blame,
When anything happens at sea.
If you ask my dear wife,
You can bet your sweet life,
It's either Our Maggie – or Me.

Douglas Walker

Age 90

BATTLE
OF THE SEXES

WHAT THE SLEEPING BEAUTY WOULD HAVE GIVEN HER RIGHT ARM FOR

This princess was different.
She was a brunette beauty with
a genius of a brain.
Refusing marriage, she
inherited all by primogenesis.
The country's economy
prospered under her rule.
When the handsome prince
came by on his white charger,
she bought it from him
and started her own
racehorse business.

Zoe Ellis

SOUTHPORT

Age 16

'OH GRAVE WHERE IS THY STING, OH LOVE, THY VICTORY?'

They were teenage
sweethearts, but he went north
to work.
Years later, revisiting the
village, he saw her in
the cemetery tending a grave.
'So you've buried three
husbands?'
'Yes, If you'd played your
cards right years ago' – pointing
to the headstone – 'your name
could have been on there
too . . .

Tom Prideaux

ST. IVES

A WALK ON THE CLIFFS

They walked together.
He, plainly admiring her,
moved closer.
She glanced at him. Repulsive!
'Please God, don't let him
touch me!'
She moved away – slipped!
The raging sea crashed
beneath her.
He clasped her hands,
grasped her body, drawing her
closer to him and safety.
'Hold me tight!' she begged.

Sylvia Still

LANCING

LOST LOVE

Prickly heat wrapped round
his head like an electric
blanket. Sweat filled his room,
a tropical greenhouse of
stale odours of a fortnight's
sloth and inactivity. Where
might she be now?
Still four hours of night.
On creased sheets lay
her letter. It was nearly
time to read it again.

John Palmer

BOURNEMOUTH

MOTHER LOVE

My stepfather was cruel.
I did not like him. We walked
by the lake, my stepfather
and I. I slipped into the water.
It was deep. I struggled.
He tried to save me, but I
pressed his head beneath the
slimy water.
We are alone again,
my Mother and I.

Kathleen Dyne

EDINBURGH

LADY GUEST
AT THE SAVOY

Culmination of a year's
determined pursuit. Gilt-edged
mirrors reflect his cufflinks, his
teeth, small leather jewellery
box on the table between
them. Champagne sings in her
ears, muffling his words . . .
'Souvenir of shared
pleasures . . . only wish
it could've been otherwise.'
Something's wrong. The
lid flips up on cultured
pearls.

Fiona Kerr

LONDON SW10

TEA FOR TWO

Eleanor, the glamorous,
vivacious actress, was amazed
to find that her late
husband's mistress was a
comfortable dowdy woman
called Muriel living in
Surbiton.
'Edward loved us both'
said Muriel 'but every
Thursday he did like a bit
of peace and quiet.'
Now Eleanor visits Muriel
every Thursday for tea.

C.J. Kennard

ASSORTED
ALIENS

ALIEN ECONOMY

The flying saucer landed
in Alf's orchard.
Alf's mower had stopped again.
The alien pointed to the apples.
Alf pointed to the mower.
The alien mended the mower.
Alf gave him some apples.
The alien left.
Alf's lawn mower gave no
more trouble and never
used another drop of petrol.

Tony Ellis

ORMSKIRK

FIRMLY IN THE FIRMAMENT

A week in space in his
escape module and now only
a few hour's air supply
remained. Then he saw it — the
largest craft he had ever
seen. Rescue! He manoeuvred
his module into the
opened hatch.
The doorway closed.
Darkness, death.
The orifice opened again,
letting out a belch.

Bryan John Holmes

HEANOR

MAN OR MANUFACTURED?

'The Spacesearcher' prepared
to leave the planet and embark
on its journey home. 'It's a
pity,' the chief biologist
sighed into the intercom,
'Humanoids . . . robots with
the ability to procreate.
But not a "natural"
being on this planet.'
A vapour trail in the sky; a
ship was leaving Earth's
atmosphere.

P. H. D'Arcy

PENZANCE

ALWAYS READ
THE SMALL PRINT

How the hell had
he ended up here? The heat,
the smell of brimstone,
and no sign of that damned
optician. Stupid gimmick,
dressed in red,
with horns and a tail.
Devilish!
He should never have signed
for his spectacles before
receiving them.
He can't read a thing
without them.

Earl J. Peacock

MITCHAM

PEOPLE ARE
THE SAME
THE UNIVERSE OVER

He was terrified when
spaceships first landed on
the hill. Slowly his
courage returned, enough
to crawl up through the
undergrowth.
Two aliens were arguing
over the flags each had
erected. Abruptly they
returned to their ships and
flew off.
The fight blazed across
the sky like a meteor
shower.

G. Kennell

NUNEATON

WHEN THE SPACE CLOUD THAT FED UPON THOUGHT ENERGY CAME TO EARTH FOR A MEAL

Religious ideas were highest
and, therefore, eaten first.
Lush fare, well hung, but
squishy with fresh blood.
Politics promised more
but disappointed.
Philosophy filled without
nourishing.
Art intoxicated without
liberating.
Individual notions of self
were identical as fish eggs
and tasteless.
After dinner a noise
thundered across the universe:
BEEEELLLCHH!

Steve King

WEYMOUTH

THE DEVIL DOESN'T ALWAYS LOOK AFTER HIS OWN

The vampire snarled
and folded his black silk
cloak around him before
slamming the coffin
lid shut.
'Just my luck' he hissed.
It had seemed a good idea to
leave his castle for Greenland
and lots of healthy unsuspecting
Eskimos.
Nobody at Transylvanian
Tours Ltd. had mentioned the
Midnight Sun.

T.K. Dawber

BLACKBURN

'FOR FRANK'

Prepared though they
were, the first sight of the
alien was still a shock.
Seventeen feet tall,
and pyramid shaped.
Three heads, two of which
were under its arms.
One square eye at the end
of each prehensile toe.
But you can't help liking
someone who wears a
pink bow-tie.

David Brazier

BEMBRIDGE

A
FRANGLAIS
SAGA

'Bonjour, mon friend!'
cried a bird – 'Je suis very
talented!' it boasted.
'Because you can talk?'
questioned the boy.
'Pas seulement that, mais je can
parler in *deux* languages,'
it answered.
'Two languages? Which ones?'
'Francais et English, mon
copain!'
'That's not French!'
he retorted.
'Mais oui!
C'est pigeon French!!'

Adrienne King

MATLOCK

Age 17

234

CHANGING
PARTNERS

THE DECEIVER

Walking hand-in-hand
in the sunshine, he stoops
and picks a flower for
her. She smiles happily,
secure in the knowledge
of his love and loyalty.

At home, loving, trusting, his
wife and children wait, happily,
secure in the knowledge of
his love and loyalty.

A timebomb is ticking.

Brenda Rogers

EAST GRINSTEAD

PILLAGE AND RAPE

Pompous Freeman Beowulf
tells his wife,
'Vikings are taking over
York. Stay at home,
busy yourself with household
duties and you need not
fear pillage or rape, I will
look after you.'
Alone, his wife thought
hard, then putting on her
favourite dress, creeps out
to join the Vikings . . .

Des Ramsay

SCARBOROUGH

A BUSINESS AFFAIR

'Infidelity is sometimes
justifiable,' James thought.
He must get that contract.
Richards was immovable,
but his wife . . . The weekend
with her was expensive but
eventually . . .
'And how was your weekend?'
he asked his wife.
'Marvellous' she answered
dreamily, 'I bumped into Mark
Richards – he gave me this
contract for you.'

B. G. Pasoua

ST OVEN, JERSEY

CONFIDENCE CONFOUNDED

Maria was about to leave
Richard. Her handsome tycoon
friend had arrived to take
her away. Richard didn't mind.
His lovely secretary would
replace Maria.
The secretary arrived
prematurely, parking
alongside the tycoon.
She smiled at him.
It was love at first sight.
They drove away
in the tycoon's car.

Gilbert Townend

LEEDS

THE CIRCLE
OF LOVE IS
STRONGEST WHEN
WE ARE FREE
TO TRAVEL ITS
OUTSIDE PERIMETER

When the child
cried she comforted him.
As the boy grew he resisted
his mother's warm embrace and
looked for affection elsewhere.
Returning in maturity, when
the strong maternal fingers
could no longer lock
in his freedom, he
felt both love
and compassion for
the first woman in his life.

R. Ann Gardner

ALLESTREE

WRITING
MINI-SAGAS

PREFACE

An interesting little
exercise, Mr Aldiss:
short stories of fifty words.
Such an economy of paper
and ink should commend
the concept to:
the Friends of the Earth;
schoolboys at their homework;
the Campers' Club;
secret scholars;
short distance commuters
and slow readers.
As a slow writer,
to me too.

A.E. Anson

HARLESTON

THE DINOSAUR ARCHBISHOP

Despite the heat,
everyone celebrated the
thousandth birthday of the
Dinosaur Archbishop of
Gonwanaland. This sage was
truly wise, truly revered.
Under his sway, there
were no nuclear wars for
seven centuries.
'He sees eternity in a
grain of sand,'
William Brontosaur said.
'And all possible universes
in fifty words . . .'

Norman Perkins

GRANTHAM

WRITING
A MINI-SAGA

Morning.
Blank paper faces
me. This is more difficult
than I thought. Time passes.
Think of a subject. Reject it.
Then another. Pause for a cup
of coffee. Still no inspiration.
Foolish of me to try and
write something like this.
Lunch time. Food for
thought? Just four
more words.

Ian Laing

LLANDUDNO JUNCTION

TIME AND TIDE
WAIT FOR NO MAN

Procrastination is my one
failing. I have many capabilities
but I shall show you them
tomorrow. I have ambitions but
also plenty of time to
fulfil them. Had I not
procrastinated I would
have written a mini-saga.
Now I find there is
no tomorrow.
Time is the eventual
winner.

Jeanette Ogbourne

SWINDON

THE LONELINESS OF THE SHORT-DISTANCE WRITER

Head between hands
the man sat overwhelmed
by the enormity of the task,
stunned by the difficulties
inherent in so small a feat,
it was inconceivable that
so novel a mind as his
could be defeated by
such a trifle.
Then picking up his pen
he wrote
these fifty words.

Peter Snell

GUILDFORD

OLD AS HIS UNIVERSE

The grey beard sat
sunning himself. He appeared
extremely ancient, and I
approached him slowly,
believing him to be real.
'How old are you, sir?'
I asked.
'Not old.' He shook his
head. Perhaps he mistook
my meaning.
'How long have you lived?'
He smiled with regret, saying
'Fifty words long.'

Maggie Edmonds

HULL

Age 15

THE THING FROM DOUBLE-SPACE OR IT BRED BETWEEN THE LINES

It crawled from
radioactive swamps. Blind,
glutinous, ravening.
GLOOSH, it went.
And GLUG.
Indiscriminately, it ate.
Boxcars, breasts, ballistic
missiles. Insatiable.
Little did it know the nature
of the world.
It delved to the foundations
of the Cosmos.
Unheeding, it gnawed,
word after word . . .
Forty-eight, CRUNCH,
Forty-nine, GOBBLE,
Fifty. PERIOD.

James Cawthorn

LONDON W 10

THE KING IS DEAD: LONG LIVE THE KING (NOT IF I CAN HELP IT)

The fairly famous author
judging a literary competition
poured himself a fresh drink
and wearily scanned yet
another card.
It was a miniature in his
own particular vein,
but incomparably more
brilliant. And it had broken
no rules.
Savagely he tore it across
and flung it in the
wastepaper basket.

R. A. Manser

LONDON SE10

APHORISM

'What do you think of
mini-sagas?' I asked him.
'I don't think of them,'
Wilde replied.
The Café Royal was crowded.
I said, confidentially.
'People say they're a minor
art-form. They get the
fever and can't stop
pouring them out.'
He smiled.
'The incontinent in search
of the inconsequent . . .'

Sheila Bullen

SHENFIELD

DIVINE
INTERVENTIONS

THROW OUT THE LIFE-LINE, SOMEONE IS SINKING TODAY

'I have always loved you,'
said the wife to the dying Saint.
'Go away,' he replied.
'I am a man of rare sanctity.
You've always bored me.'
He knelt before the Heavenly
Throne. 'Here am I, Master,
your unworthy servant.'
'Too true,' said God.
'Go away. You've always
bored me.'

Bernard Steff

BOSTON

HOMECOMING

'Good to have you back, son,'
the old man said.
'Nice to be back.'
'You've had a rough time.'
The eyes clouded with
guilt. 'Hope you don't think
I let you down.'
The younger shook his head.
'You warned me, dad. But
it wasn't the nails.
It was the kiss.'

Roger Woddis

FROM SUBLIME TO SUBLIMINAL

Dwindling funds
and a leaking roof
troubled the Parochial
Church Council.
Possibly it was imagination
that the organ voluntary
one Sunday,
sounded a little
livelier than hitherto.
The girl
whispered to her mother:
'More like,
"Raindrops keep falling
on my head".'
'Yes,' agreed Mum,
'Vicar is dropping his
hints again.'

Alfred Joseph Clough

MERSEYSIDE

ALBERT BAGSHAW'S FALL FROM GRACE: HOW THE FATE OF MILLIONS TURNED ON A SINGLE QUESTION

Albert Bagshaw's job was
lonely, but he got free transport:
he was the Fourth horseman of
the Apocalypse. Everything
he looked at died. He couldn't
find a bridge partner, nor
get served down the pub.
One day he asked God,
'How come the ruddy horse
don't die?'
God sacked him.

Frank Purcell (K24059)

HM PRISON

WORMWOOD SCRUBS

— 1985 RUNNER UP – ADULT —

255

'STORY, BUDDHA!'
(A PALINDROME)

'Thinking contentedly
through life ensures bliss.
More beauty was created
never – craftsmen, old or sick,
holy or dead men – all failed.
Only Self.'
Self only?
Failed – all men, dead or holy,
sick or old? 'Mens' craft never
creates beauty?' 'More
bliss' ensures life 'through
contentedly thinking.'
'Buddha! Story . . .'

Mark Lunn

ALDERMASTON